To my favorite angel**s**:

Marilyn + Monica

With love from

Great Grandma and
Poppy Woppy

In memory of Jack Weedn, our guardian angel—*FW*

For Layla, Rayhan & Tasneem, my three precious angels—*AYL*

Angels
© 2013 Text Alexis York Lumbard
Artwork Archivea GmbH

Book Design by Cory Steffen

Wisdom Tales is an imprint of World Wisdom, Inc.

Library of Congress Cataloging-in-Publication Data
Lumbard, Alexis York, 1981- Angels / written by Alexis York Lumbard ; illustrated by Flavia Weedn. pages cm ISBN 978-1-937786-15-1 (hardcover : alk. paper) [1. Stories in rhyme. 2. Angels--Fiction.] I. Weedn, Flavia, illustrator. II. Title.
PZ8.3.L97128Ang 2013 [E]--dc23 2013014715

Printed in China on acid-free paper
Production Date: June, 2013; Plant & Location: Printed by Everbest Printing (Guangzhou, China), Co. Ltd;
Job / Batch # 111058

For information address Wisdom Tales,
P.O. Box 2682, Bloomington, Indiana 47402-2682
www.wisdomtalespress.com

Flavia®

Artwork © Archivea GmbH

Angels

Written by Alexis York Lumbard

Illustrated by Flavia Weedn

Wisdom Tales

Angels, angels

fill the air,

coming down

from way up there.

Some are big,

some are tiny.

They're all so bright

and very shiny.

Some have blue wings,

some have white.

They fly at day,

they fly at night.

Angels of spring

who love to grow.

Angels of winter

who love the snow.

Angels who heal,

angels who sing.

Angels who watch

over everything.

Angels, angels

always near,

protecting you,

my special dear!